T0365873

THE TRUE STORY OF RALPH
THE OCEAN GROVE FISHERMAN

This book is dedicated to the men and women who sacrificed their time and effort in the rebuilding of the Ocean Grove Fishing Pier that was destroyed by the Northeast Storm, December 11, 1992.

To order additional copies of this book, contact:
Xlibris
844-714-8691
www.Xlibris.com
Orders@Xlibris.com

ISBN: Softcover   978-1-4134-0263-6
        Hardcover   978-1-4134-4181-9

Library of Congress Control Number: 2003091967

Print information available on the last page

Rev. date: 02/14/2023

THE TRUE STORY OF RALPH
THE OCEAN GROVE FISHERMAN

STORY BY CAROL EGNER
ILLUSTRATED BY JANET NICASTRO

THE STORM

Friday morning, December 11, 1992. . . a day few people living in Ocean Grove would ever forget. The Northeast storm, predicted to hit the coast, was striking at full force. The waves were already breaking against the boardwalk, and high tide was not for another three hours.

Then it happened! One of the biggest waves of the day came roaring into shore. It lifted the tiny, little, white house on the end of the fishing pier up into the air and threw it out to sea; never to be seen again. Within the next couple of hours, the rough water broke apart the boardwalk. The fishing pier, that had stood for over one hundred years, stood no more. . . except for the very far end. Never before could anyone remember such destruction.

Would the people of Ocean Grove ever see the rebuilding of their beloved fishing pier and boardwalk? There were many who did not think so.

Faith is the substance of things hoped for, the evidence of things not seen. (Hebrews 11:1)

A SIGN OF HOPE

Cleaning up after the storm was a big job. Broken boards were scattered everywhere. Sand covered all the roads near the beach. The place was a mess. With Christmas right around the corner, the people of Ocean Grove (The Grovers, as they are known) felt an unusual sense of despair. That is, until the appearance of HOPE.

Hope was in the form of a small Christmas tree that mysteriously appeared on what was left of the fishing pier. Trimmed with red bows with a hand-made gold star on top, it was tied to one of the pilings. The tree was a monument to the human spirit. Some thought it was the most beautiful Christmas tree they ever saw.

THE SUMMER OF 1993

The summer of 1993 was very similar to any summer at the beach in Ocean Grove, except there was no boardwalk. No one realized how much they loved the boardwalk until it was gone. The empty platform at the end of what used to be the fishing pier, stood as a reminder to the Grovers of the tiny, little, white house that used to be there. Then another SIGN OF HOPE mysteriously appeared. It was the American Flag flying once again over the end of the Ocean Grove fishing pier.

One day, two good friends, Bob and Carol, sat on the beach admiring the flag. Suddenly they got an idea. Neither Bob nor Carol could imagine a whole summer going by without anyone fishing off the pier. It had been such a tradition in the Grove. Wouldn't it be funny to make a dummy and put him on the vacant platform with a fishing pole in his hand? Everyone would think that someone had climbed up there and was fishing. Bob and Carol laughed out loud at the thought of this.

At that moment they realized that they would have to mastermind this plan. And so began a project that they would remember for the rest of their lives.

THE MAKING OF RALPH

The next day Bob and Carol began collecting the materials they needed to make a dummy. The head was made of chicken wire which was wrapped in papier-mache. Carol painted two round balls to look like eyes and they were glued into the head. White hair was glued on to the face to look like hair and a beard. Carol made a navy blue hat for the top of the dummy's head. The face was then painted. Bob cut and screwed together a two-by-four to support the head and the body. The body was made out of chicken wire. Next, Bob and Carol had to dress the dummy.

Bob donated a pair of his old shoes and a tan pair of pants. Carol looked through her closet and found a navy blue and white striped shirt, a sleeveless red vest, and a pair of red socks. The dummy was dressed and completed.

Both Bob and Carol thought they had done a good job making him. He was really cute. Bob named him Ralph and said that Ralph's name stood for "**R**ising **A**bove the **L**ong **P**ier of **H**ope." Next, they had to figure out how to get Ralph onto the remains of the old fishing pier.

THE BIG PLAN

After hours of arguing and discussing (and I do mean arguing!), the plan to put Ralph on the fishing pier was completed. Because there was no way to get onto the remains of the fishing pier, Bob would have to make a ladder going up one of the old pilings. When he got to the top, he would lower a rope to hoist up Ralph who would be wrapped up in a plastic bag so he wouldn't get wet. A bucket was filled with the supplies they would need: an electric screwdriver, fishing line, a sinker, and fishing pole. This would also be hoisted up. Carol would then climb up the ladder. When they got to the top, Bob would secure Ralph to the pier, while Carol got his fishing pole ready.

Thursday night, July 29, 1993, was chosen because the tides would be very low. At 3:00 in the morning they would leave from Carol's house.

The night finally came when they put their plan into action, and a beautiful crystal-clear night it was! Thousands of stars filled the sky.

Bob waded out into the water first and began hammering the planks of wood onto the pilings. The hammering could be heard throughout the quiet town of Ocean Grove. Higher and higher he climbed until he finally reached the top. Carol waded out to the ladder Bob had made. Holding Ralph above her head, big waves crashed against her face. The rope was lowered to hoist up Ralph, the bucket of tools, and finally Carol.

Bob and Carol began to work quickly, securing Ralph and his fishing pole. After what seemed to be an eternity, the job was done. Ralph looked so real. Each time a wave came in, it pulled the sinker, which pulled the fishing line, which made Ralph's pole bend. Ralph really looked like he was fishing.

It is not exactly known when it happened, or how. Maybe when they looked up in the sky and saw a shooting star go by, but Ralph was given a soul. . . and he began to LIVE.

Bob and Carol climbed down leaving their friend. As they left the beach, they vowed that they would tell no one what had happened that night.

THE NEXT DAY

Early the next morning, the word went out.

"Get the police down to the Ocean Grove beach immediately!!! Someone has climbed up the fishing pier and is fishing."

The policemen called out to Ralph, "You up there, come down here immediately!" Ralph just sat there laughing to himself. The lifeguards were also fooled by Ralph.

"Hey Mister," Matt cried out, "You come down here right now." Ralph once again chuckled to himself. All day long this went on. Everyone on the beach that day wanted to know how that guy got up there. And Ralph continued to fool everyone for the rest of the summer.

In fact, Ralph sat up there and guarded the fishing pier for the next few months. Summer turned to fall, and fall to winter. Ralph decided that no matter how bad the weather was, he would not give up. Everyone needs a purpose in life, and Ralph knew that his purpose was to guard the pier and give hope. And so he did.

There were twenty-five storms that winter, some very severe. Many a morning Carol would drive down to the beach and make sure Ralph made it through the night. She was relieved to see him sitting up there next to the American Flag. More and more people came to know Ralph. The people of Ocean Grove actually began to love him. Ralph sensed his importance and was more determined than ever to remain loyal to his job.

Winter turned to spring, and heavy building equipment was brought down to the beach to rebuild the boardwalk and fix the pier. Ralph was concerned about what would happen to him. He loved doing what he was doing. It was all that mattered to him.

As time went on, Ralph became more worried that his days on the fishing pier were numbered. Then one day, the big crane that was used to pick up heavy pieces of wood was coming right down on his head.

"This is it. . . the end of me," Ralph thought. With that, the crane lifted Ralph off the spot where he had sat for almost a year. Within seconds, he was dropped into the ocean. "After all that I've done, no one cares about me. Are they just going to throw me away?"

Ralph didn't see Mrs. Layton and Mrs. Johnson, but they saw him. It's a good thing, because they had their hearts set on saving him. The waves pushed Ralph close to the beach where the two elderly ladies fished him out. Ralph was saved!

Eventually, Ralph was returned to Carol's house where she put him back together and made him look like new. For a long time, he just sat on Carol's porch thinking. Ralph wondered if he would ever be returned to the fishing pier, where he really longed to be.

It was July 4th and lo and behold, Ralph was once again being moved. Where were Bob and Carol taking him now? To a parade? Yes! He was going to ride through Ocean Grove on a float that looked just like the fishing pier.

The parade began, and Ralph rode through the town of Ocean Grove. People everywhere smiled and waved at him and were happy to see him. They even knew him by name. Ralph was so happy to see all his friends again. As the parade ended, Ralph once again wondered if he would ever see the fishing pier. Oh, to sit upon it and feel the warm sun beating down. To watch the swimming, the surfing, and the sun-bathers. To throw a line in the water and wish for a fish to bite.

Bob and Carol took Ralph down off the parade float and headed toward the beach. As they approached the boardwalk, Ralph looked out in the ocean, and there stood a beautiful, new fishing pier with the tiny, little, white house on the very end. His prayers were answered. He was returning to the one place he longed to be.

As Bob secured him to his new spot, Ralph thought he would burst with joy. He was so happy he began singing a little song. "Oh, what a wonderful life I have, sitting on the pier in my fishing hat. Everyday, feeling so fine, oh, what a wonderful life is mine."

If you ever decide to visit Ocean Grove, stop by the beach and say hello to Ralph. He will be sitting on the end of the fishing pier watching all the goings on.

And remember this. When things seem hopeless, they never really are. Always believe that it will get better. Get hooked on HOPE. HOPE is catching.

The Ralph Song

Music by Mike Boniello
Lyrics by Bob Borders